The M
Clothes

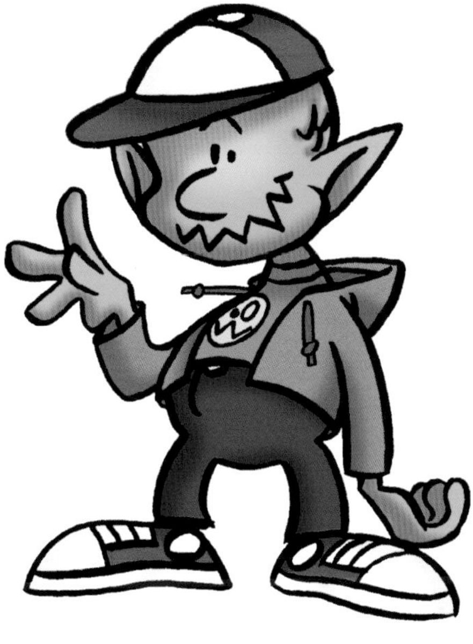

Illustrated by Alan Cochrane

Rigby

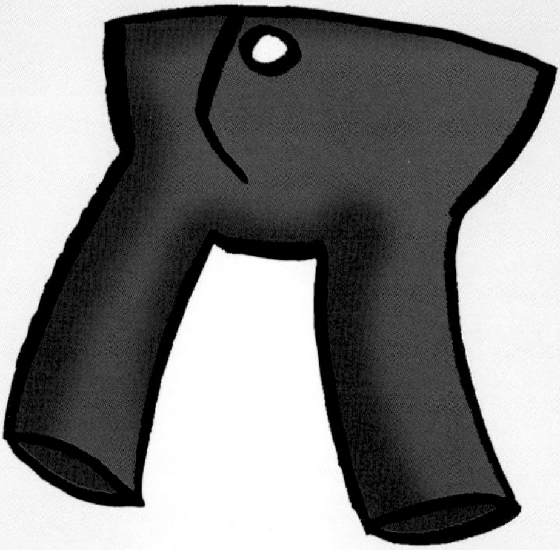

the pants

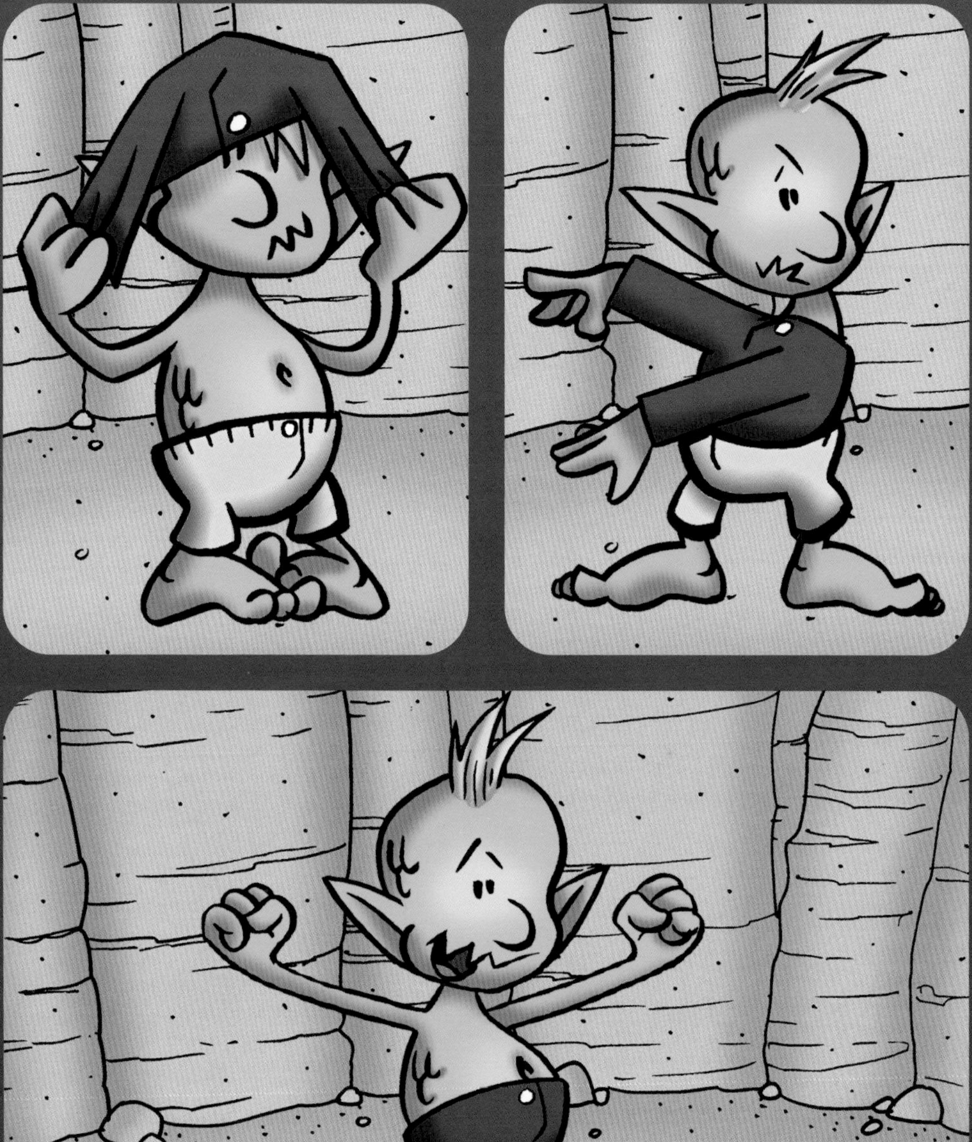

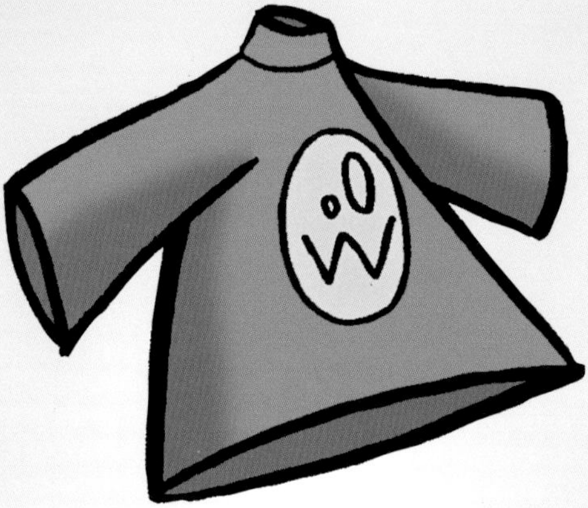

the shirt

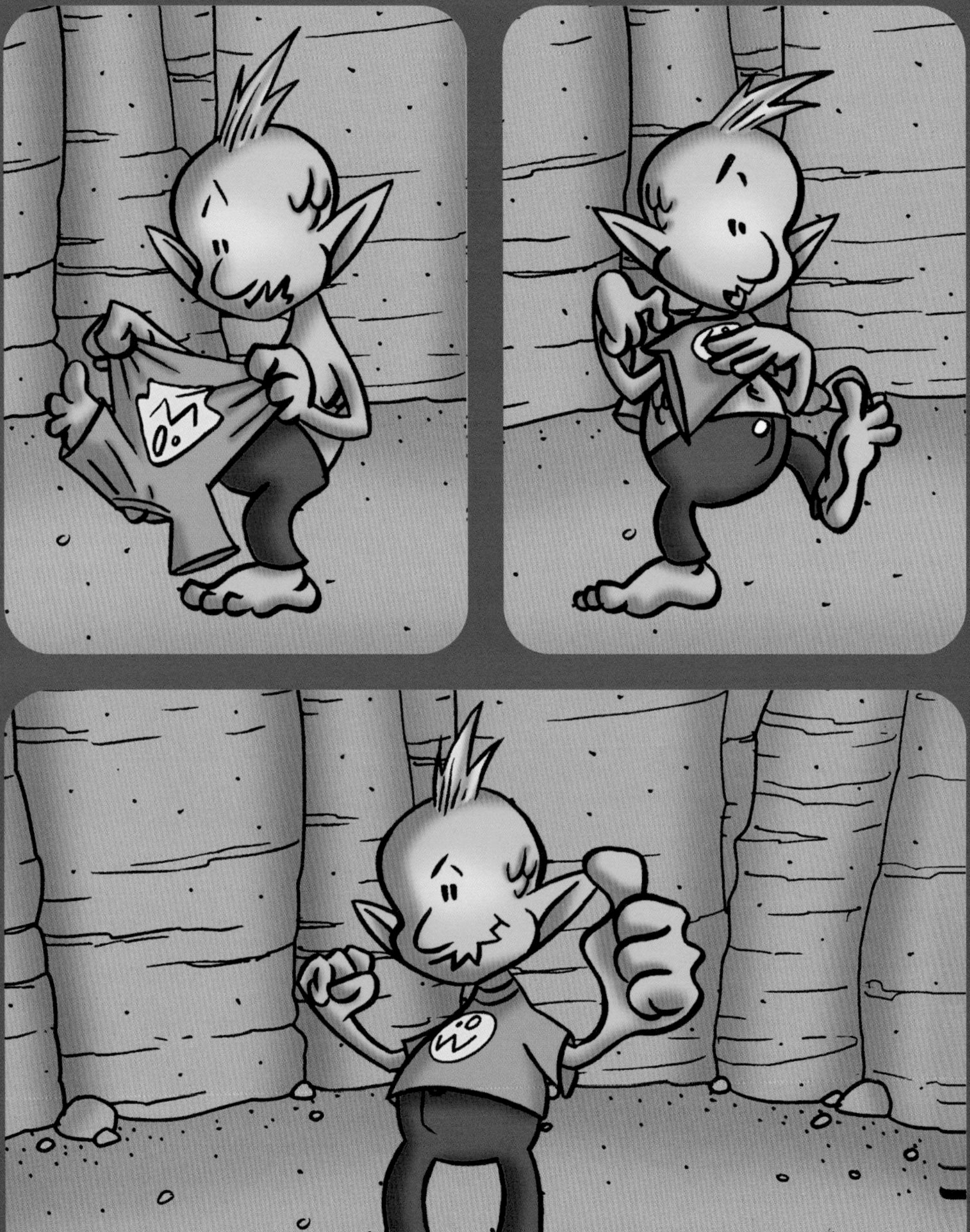

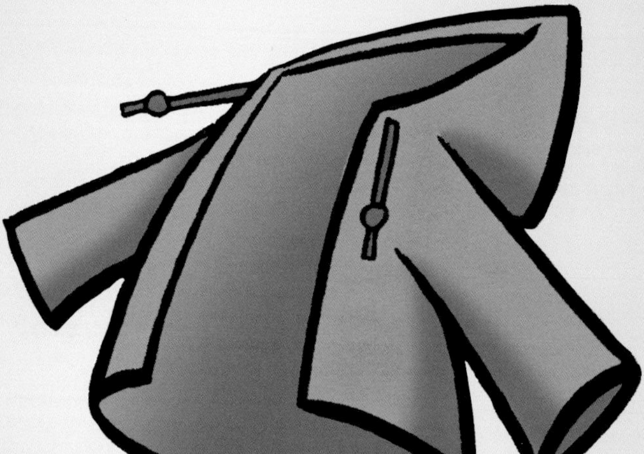

the coat

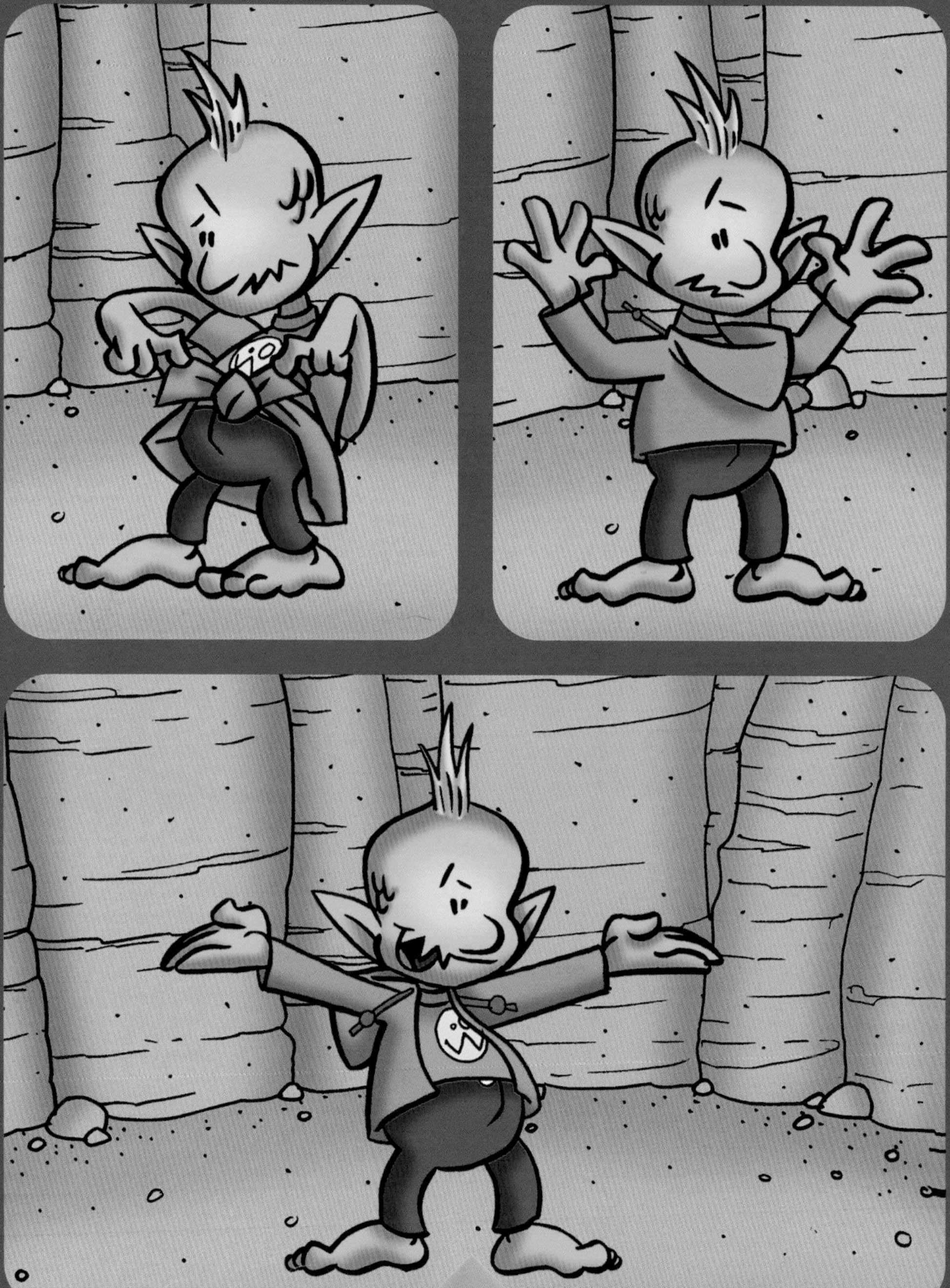

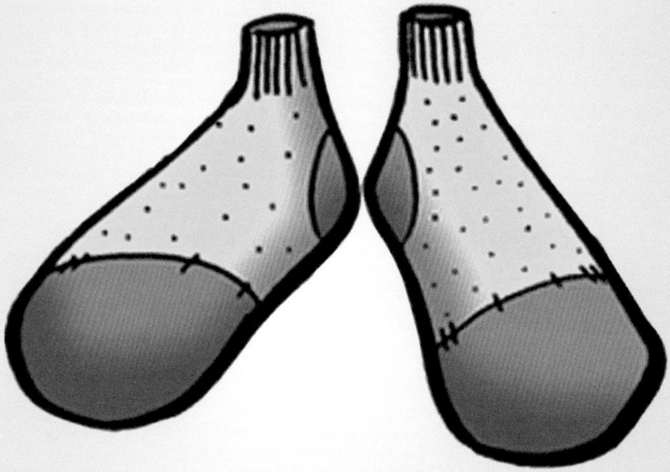

the socks

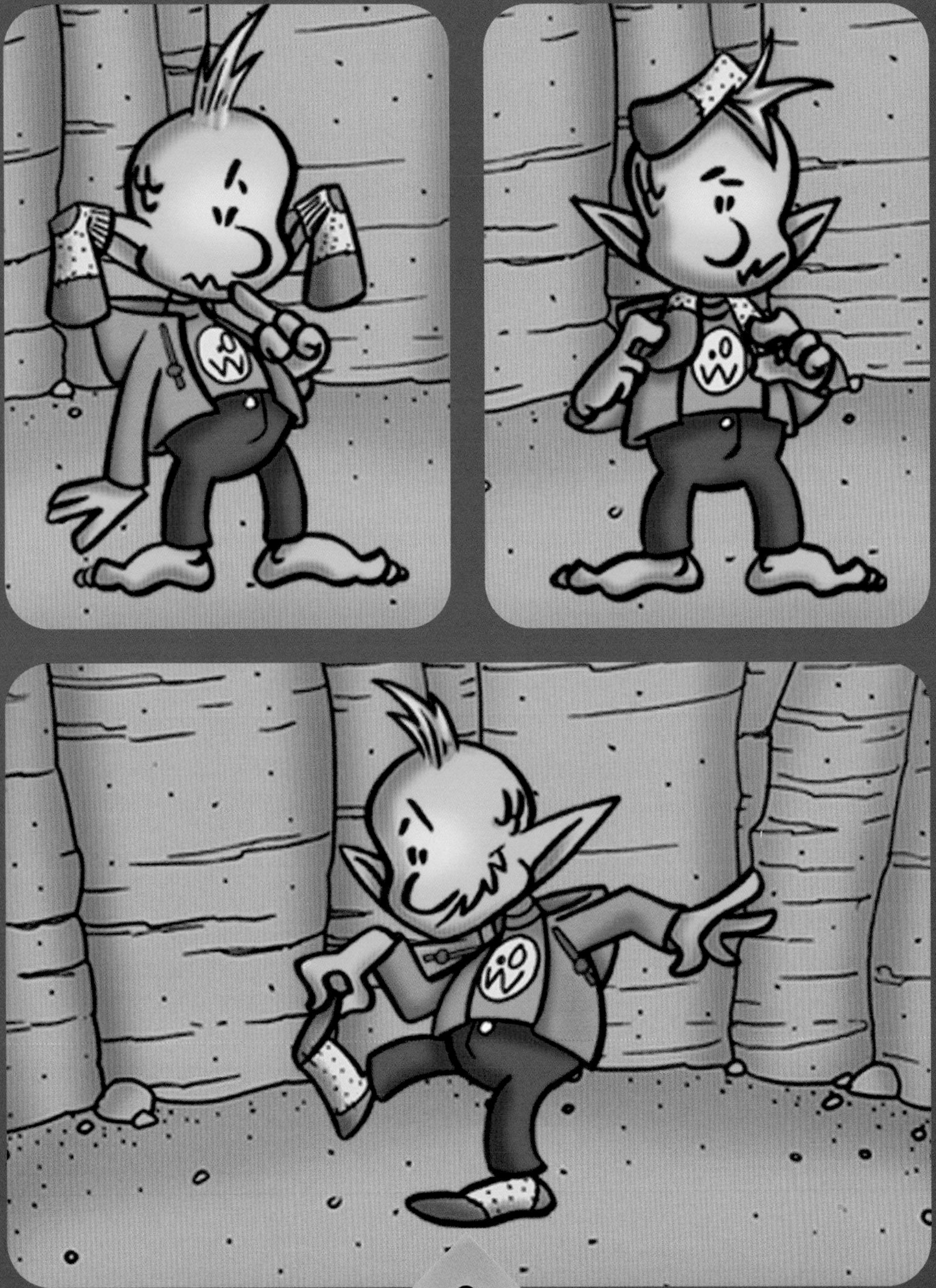

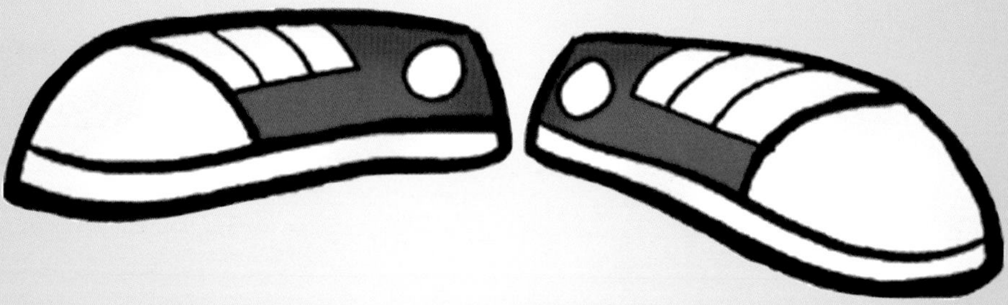

the shoes

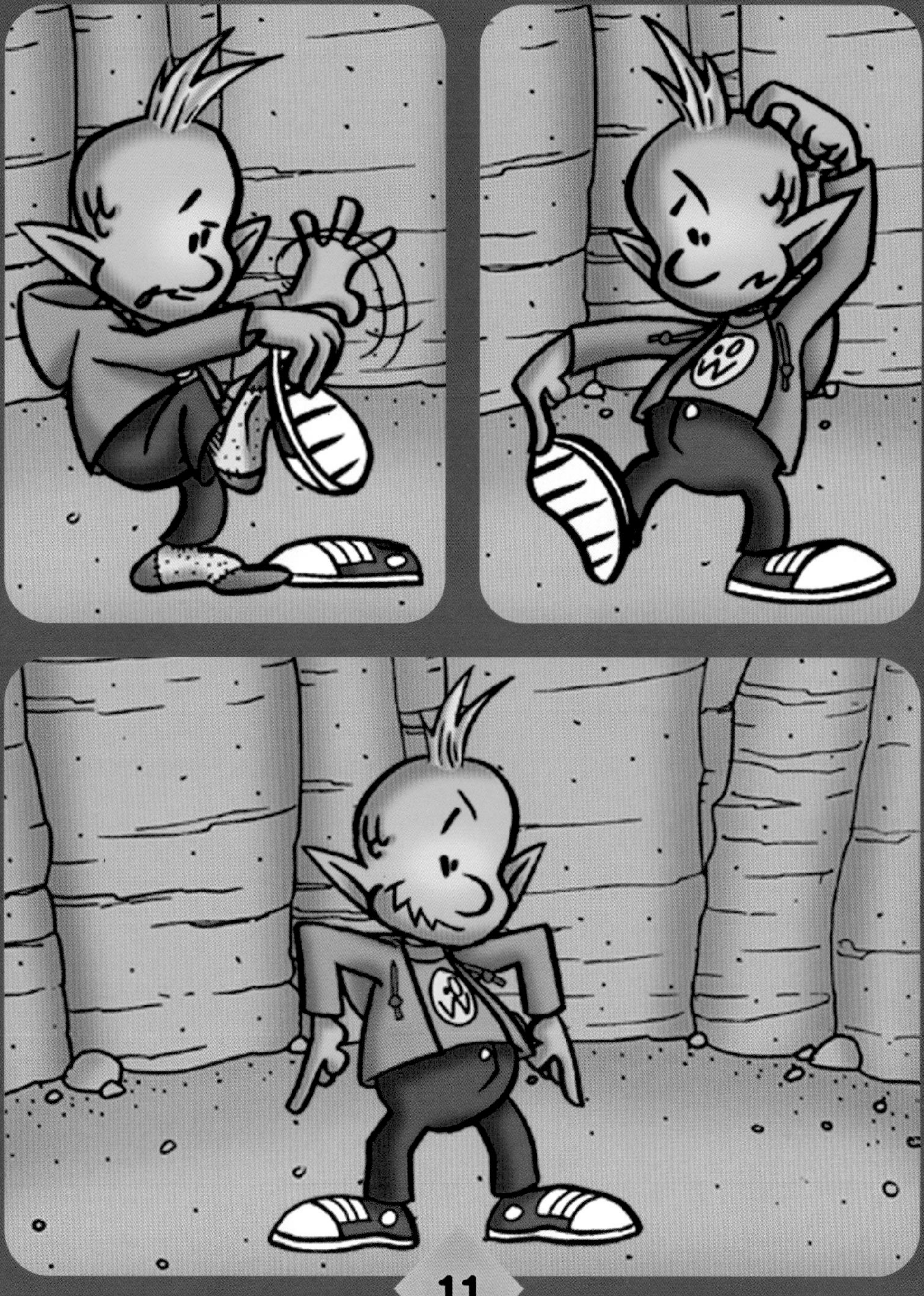

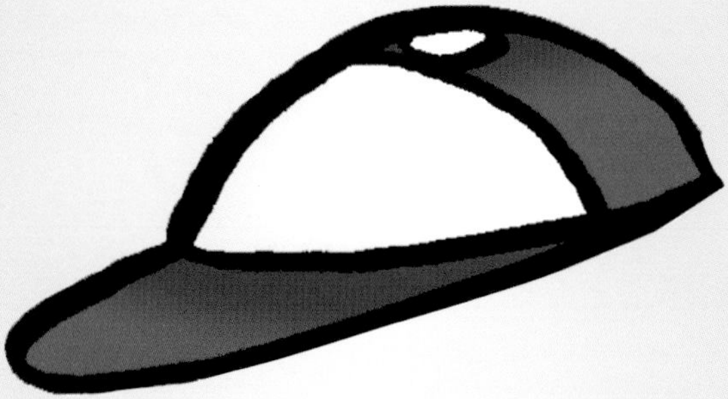

the cap

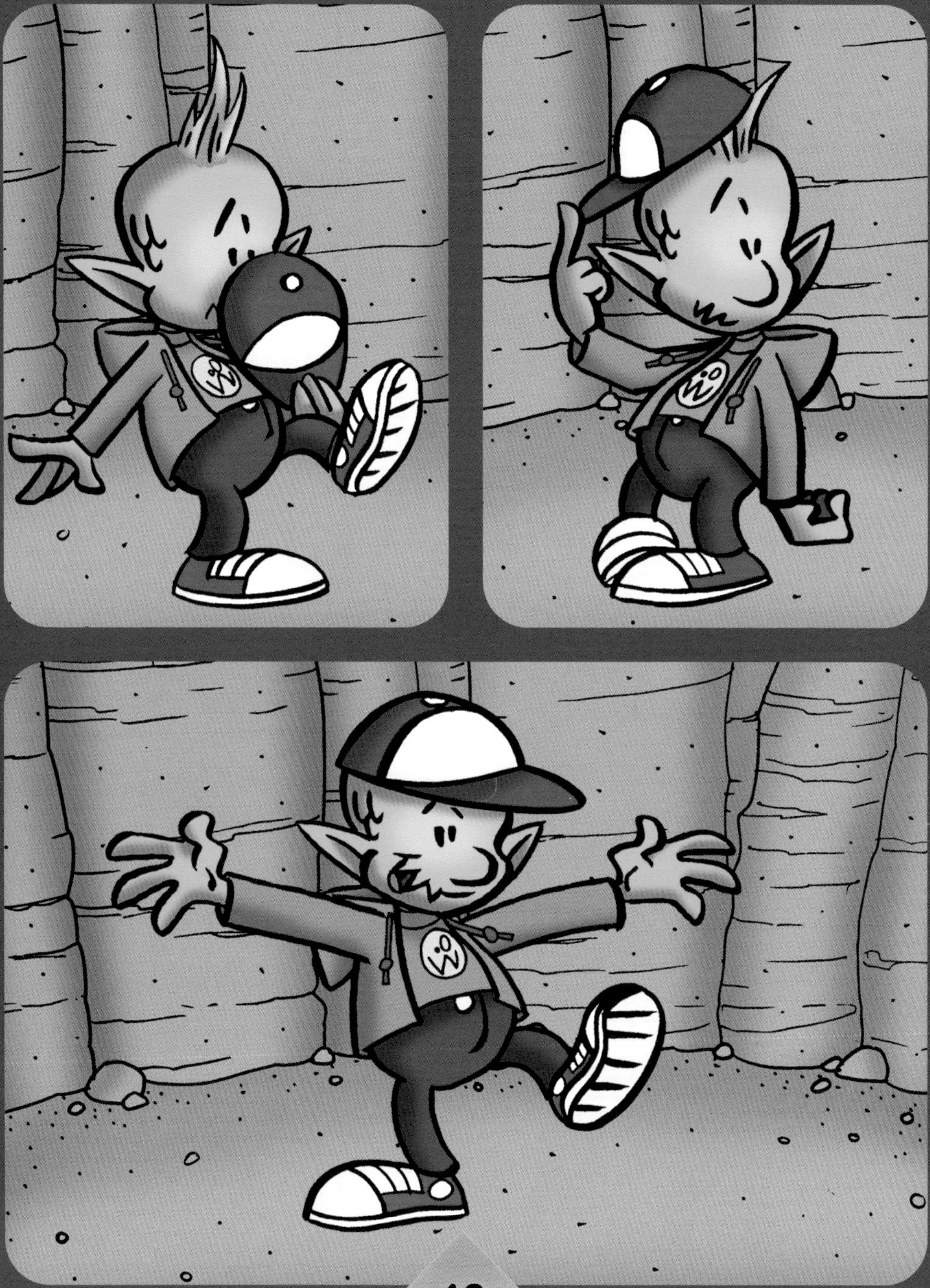

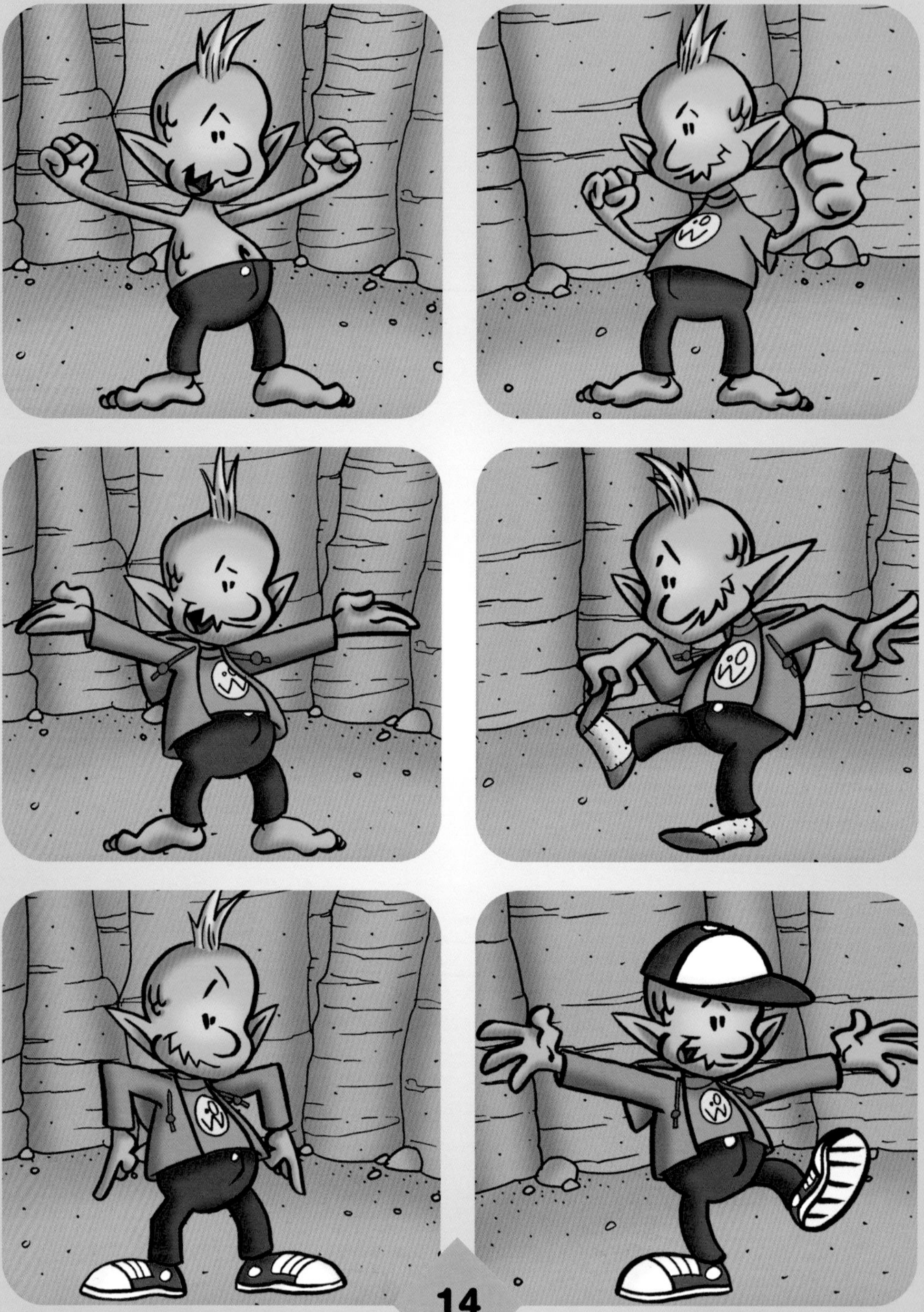

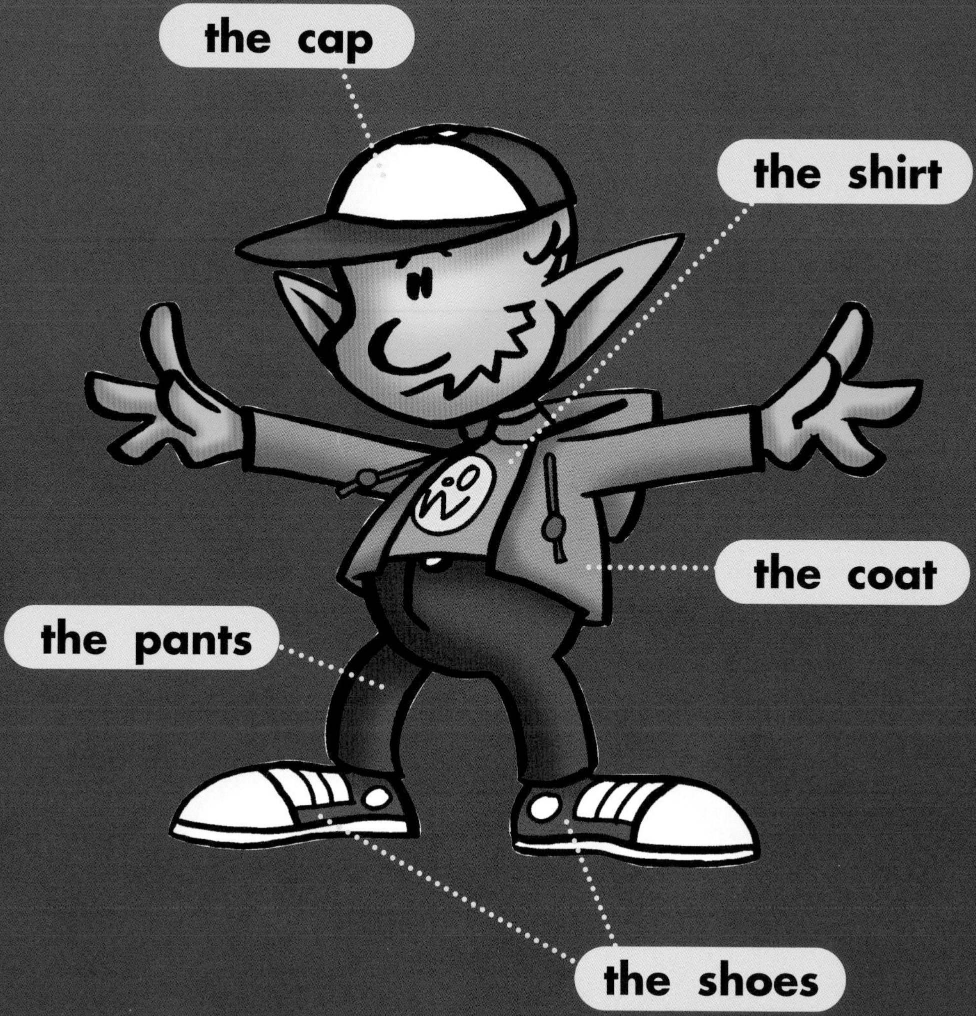
the cap
the shirt
the coat
the pants
the shoes

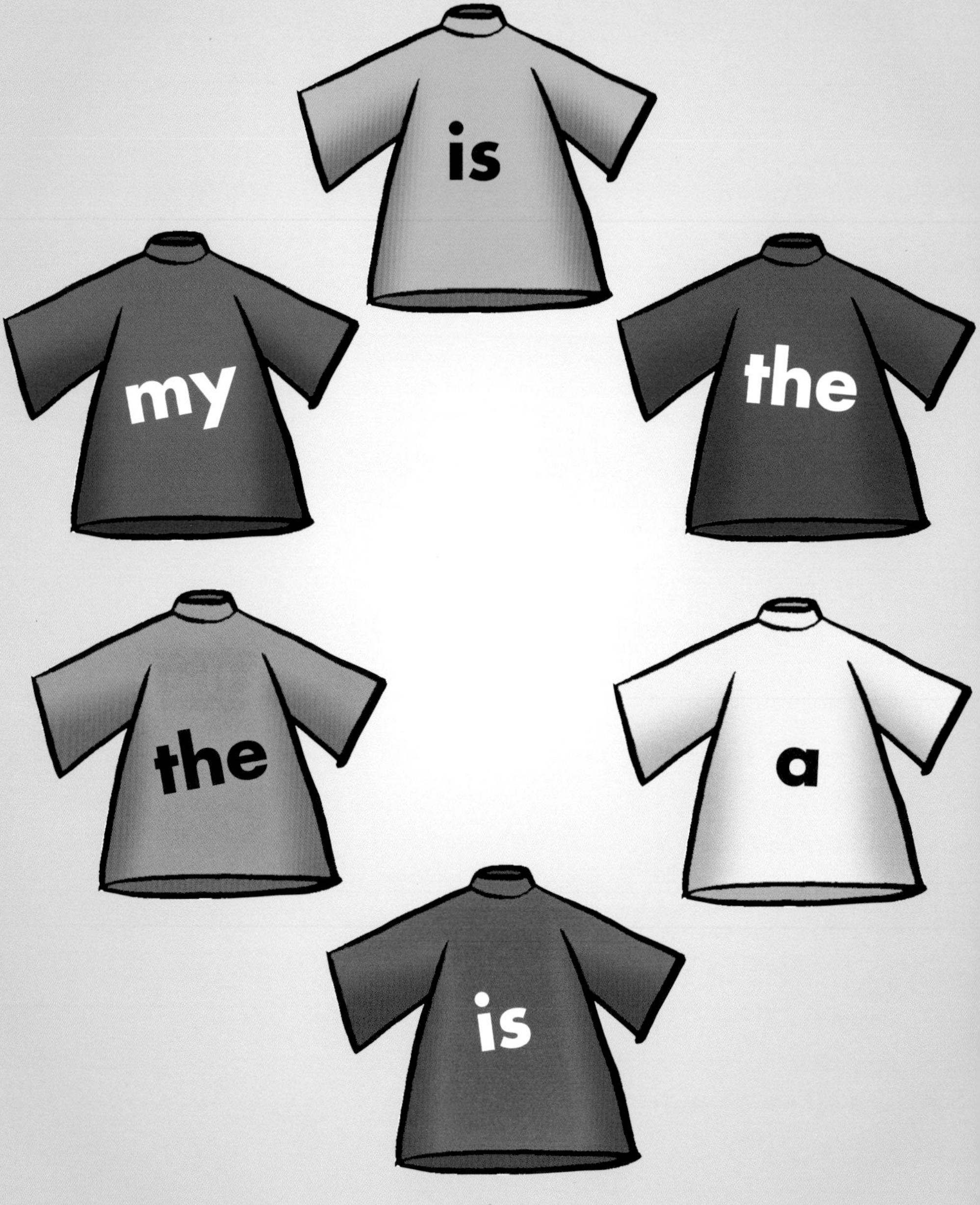
is
my
the
the
a
is